JEREMY STRONG

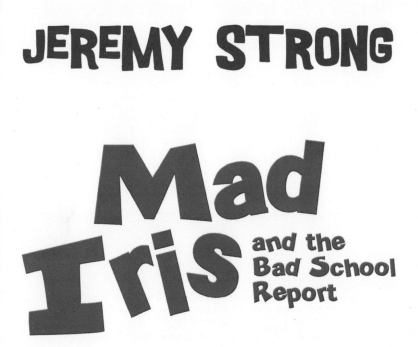

Mad
Iris and the Bad School Report

With illustrations by
Scoular Anderson

This is for Beth.
May all your three ostriches fly – just like their
mother, who flies beautifully.

First published in 2015 in Great Britain by
Barrington Stoke Ltd
18 Walker Street, Edinburgh, EH3 7LP

www.barringtonstoke.co.uk

Text © 2015 Jeremy Strong
Illustrations © 2015 Scoular Anderson

The moral right of Jeremy Strong and Scoular Anderson to
be identified as the author and illustrator of this work has
been asserted in accordance with the Copyright, Designs and
Patents Act, 1988

A CIP catalogue record for this book is available
from the British Library upon request

ISBN: 978-1-78112-506-9

Printed in China by Leo

Contents

Chapter 1
The Animal Man

Everyone in Pudding Lane School thought it was a great idea. In a few days' time a special visitor would be coming to the school. Captain Kapow the Animal Man was going to give a talk about animals to the whole school. He was going to bring some REAL animals with him.

Captain Kapow was very exciting. He always wrote his name like this –

CAPTAIN KAPOW!!

With capital letters and two exclamation marks to show how exciting he was.

The Year 1s and 2s were 100% certain that Captain Kapow would bring a real giraffe.

The Year 3s and 4s were far more sensible. Anyone could see giraffes were too tall for school. They knew for sure that Captain Kapow would bring a lion.

The Year 5s and 6s told the younger children that there was no way Captain Kapow would bring a lion into school. But they had heard that he had a spitting cobra.

"What's a spitting cobra?" a worried Year 2 asked.

"It's a snake that spits poison at you – SPLLARGH! Like that," Ian Tufnell said. Ian liked to scare people. He did a good job of scaring the Year 2. She burst into tears and said she'd gone off Captain Kapow and his animals and she wanted her teddy.

In fact, none of the children really knew what animals Captain Kapow would bring with him. It was a funny thing, but it was more exciting *not* to know. In any case, the head teacher, Mr Grimble, had exciting plans of his own. He told everyone in Assembly.

"I want you to collect as many cardboard boxes as you can," Mr Grimble told the children. "They can be any shape and size – tiny ones, small ones, big ones, *massive* ones. They will all be useful. We will use them to make some life-sized model animals. When Captain Kapow sees them he will be very impressed and think we are the best school in the country."

"In the world!" young Max shouted. He was only just five and liked to call out in Assembly.

"Yes, Max," Mr Grimble agreed. "The best school in the world. Now –"

"In the universe!" Max yelled before Mr Grimble could go on.

"Yes, Max," the head teacher said, and his face turned bright red. "In the universe. Please don't call out in Assembly."

The older children started to snigger. They liked it when Max shouted out things and made Mr Grimble go red.

"Every class will make their own display of animals," Mr Grimble said. "We'll put some of the best ones in the hall where everyone can see them."

"Even aliens!" Max called out.

"Not aliens, I don't think, Max." Mr Grimble sighed, but he was smiling a secret smile to himself. He said a few more things about Captain Kapow and then he told the children to go back to their classrooms.

Of course everyone was busy talking about what animals they would like to make models of.

Ross and Katie were in Mrs Norton's class. They were good friends – very good friends. Some people said that Katie was Ross's girlfriend. Ross said NO SHE WAS NOT, but just like Mr Grimble, he said it with a secret smile. (People don't always say what they are really feeling!)

"I think we should make an ostrich," Gloria said.

"We've already got an ostrich, a real one," Kelly Jessup snapped.

That was quite true. Pudding Lane School *did* have a real ostrich. Her name was Mad Iris. Mad Iris had escaped from an ostrich farm. She'd come to live at the school and the school had adopted her as their mascot.

Everyone loved Mad Iris even when she stole their packed lunches and ate them. Sometimes she ate their gym shoes too, or their ties, or their socks. Once she ate Ross's swimming trunks, and the phone in the school office. Ostriches will eat almost *anything*.

Mrs Norton, the class teacher, had an idea of her own.

"We are going to build the biggest land animal there is!" she said.

The class boggled. The biggest land animal of all? That could only mean one thing. They were going to make an elephant!

Chapter 2

The Woman with Four Feet

The next morning Mr Grimble stood at his office window. He was looking at a rather odd sight outside. First of all there came a parade of children carrying cardboard boxes. Some of the boxes were so big they hid the child carrying them. All Mr Grimble could see was the box and a pair of small feet.

There was something even odder behind the children. Mr Grimble watched as a strange creature walked up the path to the school door.

7

It looked like a woman, but she was a very funny shape. She was bulgy and she had four feet. Yes, Mr Grimble counted them again. It was a bulgy woman with two big feet and two small ones. That made four in total.

A few moments later there was a knock at Mr Grimble's office door. The secretary, Mrs Perch, poked her head round the door. Mrs Perch looked a bit alarmed, but then Mrs Perch often looked a bit alarmed. Even the office computer scared her.

"There's a Mrs Fretting here to see you, Mr Grimble," Mrs Perch announced.

"Fine, fine. Send her in, Mrs Perch," said Mr Grimble.

Mrs Fretting was the woman with four feet. She almost jumped past the door, as if she thought the door might take a sudden snap at her. When she was safely in the room, Mrs Fretting opened her extra-large coat. Under

the coat was a small child with a pale, rather blank face and ears that stuck out.

"This is Charlie," Mrs Fretting said.

"Hello, Charlie, pleased to meet you," said Mr Grimble. Charlie looked at Mr Grimble, then at his mother, and then at the head teacher again.

"I want Charlie to come to your school," Mrs Fretting said. "We have just moved to the area. My neighbour said your school was a good one."

"Oh, thank you," Mr Grimble said. "We like to think it is."

"The thing is, Charlie has problems," said Mrs Fretting. "He's allergic. He's got lots of allergies."

Charlie looked at his mum and then at Mr Grimble. His thin face was blank.

"Oh dear," Mr Grimble murmured. "Just what is Charlie allergic to?"

"Doors," Charlie's mother said.

"Doors?" said Mr Grimble. He was rather surprised, to say the least.

"Yes. They attack him," Mrs Fretting declared.

"Do you mean he bumps into them, that sort of thing?" Mr Grimble said.

"No. They attack him," Mrs Fretting insisted. "They come flying at him."

Mr Grimble cleared his throat. "I really don't think doors can fly," he said.

Mrs Fretting ignored the head teacher. "I have to keep Charlie under my coat when we go in or out a door, or he comes up in bruises and bumps. And he's got other allergies too. He's allergic to books and to reading."

"Oh dear," Mr Grimble said with a big sigh. He could see that being allergic to reading could be very awkward in a school – or anywhere else for that matter.

"Yes," said Mrs Fretting. She nodded hard. "You put a book in front of Charlie and it sets him off. He just sneezes and sneezes. Sometimes I'm surprised he's still got a nose on his face."

"Oh dear," Mr Grimble repeated. He looked at Charlie again. Charlie's face still had no expression on it at all. He simply looked back at Mr Grimble and then at his mother as if he was waiting to see what would happen next.

"And there's one more thing he's allergic to," Mrs Fretting went on. "Ostriches. You don't have any ostriches in the school, do you?"

"Ostriches?" Mr Grimble bit his lip. Oh dear. This was getting difficult. He needed more pupils for the school. And there was something about Charlie that interested Mr Grimble. He had an odd mother for a start. Mr Grimble knew that sometimes parents said things about their child that weren't *exactly* true. The child was not always who the parent thought they were.

But there *was* an ostrich in Pudding Lane School. Mad Iris. What on earth should Mr Grimble say to Mrs Fretting?

Mr Grimble stood up from his chair and beamed a smile at Mrs Fretting and Charlie. "I'm happy to say we do *not* have an ostrich here, Mrs Fretting," he said.

Of course, Mr Grimble was right. He didn't have an ostrich *here*. That was because the ostrich was in the caretaker's shed, over *there*, where she lived, on the other side of the school.

Mr Grimble was also crossing his fingers behind his back.

"We would love to have Charlie at our school and I am sure he will be very happy here," said Mr Grimble. His fingers were still crossed behind his back.

"Good," Mrs Fretting said. "Just be careful with doors. Cover him up when he goes in or out of one. And keep him away from the library and all them nasty books."

"Right," Mr Grimble said with a nod. "We'll do our best."

Charlie looked at his mum and then he looked at the head teacher, just as before. His face was still an empty sheet of paper.

Chapter 3

Bad News

Mr Grimble put Charlie in Mrs Norton's class. Mrs Norton asked Ross and Katie to help look after him until he got used to the school. Ross was surprised when Mrs Norton told him to make sure Charlie was covered with a coat when he went in or out of the door.

"He's allergic to doors," Mrs Norton explained.

Ross was even more surprised when Charlie refused to hide under Ross's coat. Instead he walked in and out of all the doors in the school and didn't bat an eyelid.

"But you're allergic to doors," Ross said. He wondered if Charlie would come out in spots, or maybe explode.

"No." Charlie shook his head. "My mum thinks I'm allergic to doors, but I'm not. Look."

Charlie walked out of the door, turned round, came back and walked in again. He did that ten times and each time he got past the door he made his eyes boggle. He stuck out his arms, waggled his fingers at Ross and Katie and went "YAAAAA!" in glee.

"When I was three I walked into a door by mistake," Charlie explained. "I got a black eye. Mum thought I was half dead and took me to the hospital. I was OK of course. But ever since then she's been telling people I'm allergic to doors. She also thinks I'm allergic to reading," he went on. "But I love books. And one day my grandad read me a story about an ostrich and I had a sneezing fit. Then Mum started to tell people I'm allergic to ostriches *and* reading, but I'm not. Anyway, I've never even seen a real ostrich."

"We can show you one!" Katie shouted. "Follow me!"

Ross and Charlie trailed after Katie.

"Your mum's weird," Ross told Charlie.

Charlie shrugged. "I think everyone is weird in some way."

"I'm not," Ross said with a laugh.

"Yes you are," Charlie said. "For example, anyone can see you like Katie a lot, but you pretend not to. Why? If I liked Katie I'd want to tell everyone."

Ross frowned. Hmmm. Was Charlie right?
He *did* like Katie, but he didn't know that
people could tell.

"How do you know I like Katie?" he said.

For the first time Charlie's face broke into
a smile. "You look at her as if you want to hold
hands with her all the time."

"I don't!" Ross snapped.

"Yes you do," Katie said with a giggle.
"Gloria's noticed and Kelly and, well, just about
the whole class. Even Mrs Norton knows."

"Mrs Norton!" Ross choked.

This was too much! Ross told himself that
he'd never look at Katie again, but then of
course he looked right at her. He had to. He
did like Katie. But Charlie was the first person
Ross had met who didn't seem to think it
mattered. Ross had a lot to think about.

By this time Katie was dragging both Ross and Charlie across to meet Mad Iris. Katie was desperate to see if Charlie would break out in spots or sneeze all over the place.

But it turned out that Mad Iris liked Charlie almost as much as Ross liked Katie.

She stuck her head down his shirt.

She twiddled his hair with her beak.

And then she undid his laces and tried to eat his shoes.

"She's lovely," Charlie said, and his pale face lit up with a huge grin. He liked all the attention he was getting from this strange bird. He didn't sneeze and he didn't explode either. He did cough a couple of times, but that was because Mad Iris had just butted him in the stomach with her head, twice.

"She does that when she likes someone," Katie said with a proud smile as Mad Iris did the same to her and Ross.

"It's her way of saying 'thank you'," Ross explained. "We saved her from the ostrich farm. She ran away and then some men came to catch her and turn her into ostrich steaks, but Katie and I saved her. Then Mr Grimble said the school could keep her."

"Here comes Mr Grimble now," Katie said. "He doesn't look very happy, does he?"

Mr Grimble did not look happy at all. In fact, the children had never seen him looking so upset.

"Are you all right, Mr Grimble?" Ross asked.

"No. I am not all right, Ross, but thank you for asking," Mr Grimble said. "I have just had some bad news. Very bad news. Inspectors are coming to the school."

"Police inspectors?" Charlie said. "Exciting!"

"No, Charlie. I'd be delighted if they were police inspectors," Mr Grimble said. He had turned as pasty white as spilled milk. "No. These are school inspectors. Three inspectors are coming to inspect our school. And then write a report about us. Oh dear. Oh dear, oh dear. Inspectors. Here, in our school!"

Charlie raised his eyebrows and looked at the others. "I think our head teacher is allergic to school inspectors," he said.

Chapter 4
Bamboo Shoots

There were three inspectors. Mr Grimble introduced them to the children in Assembly.

Miss Cactus was in charge. She had on a black dress and a black, dangerous look in her eyes that could turn you into stone at ten paces. Her top half was thin and her bottom half was wide, so she looked like a black pyramid with legs. Miss Cactus liked to ask awkward questions like, "What is a platypus?"

Gloria put up her hand and asked Miss Cactus if it was a cat that had been run over. Miss Cactus said of course it wasn't and was Gloria trying to be funny? Gloria said she didn't think a squashed cat was the least bit funny.

"Then why did you say it?" Miss Cactus snapped.

Gloria turned bright red, hung her head and stared at her knees. Her knees were a lot kinder to look at than Miss Cactus's face.

Mr Singh had a beard and a turban. When he smiled his big, friendly smile, it showed two gold teeth, one next to the other. He kept a photo of his five children in his jacket pocket.

"These are my children," he told the Assembly with pride. "They are good children. Are *you* good children?"

Ross opened his mouth to say he was good but then he stopped. Just because *he* thought something it didn't mean everyone else thought the same way. After all, sometimes he got into trouble with Mrs Norton. Maybe Mrs Norton didn't think Ross was good. Ross decided it was best to keep quiet, so he did.

Mr Singh smiled. He put the photo back in his jacket pocket and patted it a few times.

The third inspector was called Mr Twine and he was tall and very thin. The sleeves of his jacket were too short, so you could see his bony hands and wrists. Mr Twine didn't say much at all except "Ah!" or "Oh!" or "Hmmmm". He seemed to look at the ceiling a lot. Ross wondered if he was a ceiling inspector.

After Assembly, Ross and his friends went back to their classroom. Mrs Norton told them that they were going to make a start on building a cardboard elephant.

"We have lots of boxes," she said. "Well done, everybody. I would like you all to get into your groups."

Mrs Norton sometimes split the class into four groups to do things like P.E. She had given each group a name. They were Cabbages, Peas, Beans and Broccoli. Mrs Norton thought that if the children were named after vegetables they might like eating vegetables more. So far the idea didn't seem to be working, but Mrs Norton carried on all the same.

"Now then, I would like Peas and Beans to build the legs," Mrs Norton said.

Ian Tufnell's hand shot up. He was in the Peas group. "Please, Miss," he said, "the Beans smell."

Everyone burst out laughing, even half the Beans.

"No we don't!" they giggled.

Mrs Norton sighed. "Just get on with it," she ordered. "Broccoli, you can make the body, and Cabbages, you can make the trunk. There."

So that was sorted. Mrs Norton went and sat down. She hoped that the elephant would keep them busy for at least half an hour. But just as they got started, the three inspectors marched in.

"What's going on here?" Miss Cactus asked.

"We're making an elephant," Kelly Jessup told her.

"Why?" Miss Cactus demanded.

"Captain Kapow is coming tomorrow," several children chanted. "He's bringing real live animals!"

"I see," Miss Cactus murmured. She pursed her lips. "Will he bring an elephant with him?"

"I think that's rather unlikely," Mrs Norton said with a chuckle.

"Then why make one?" Miss Cactus smiled as if she had just laid a careful trap and it had worked. She had just caught Mrs Norton and a whole class in it.

"Are you going to measure it? Weigh it? Write about it? Do you know what elephants eat?" Miss Cactus asked. She glared at the class.

Ian Tufnell's hand shot up. "Bamboo shoots!" he shouted.

Mrs Norton groaned.

Miss Cactus groaned.

Mr Singh gave a sad smile.

And Mr Twine said, "Oh!" and he looked at the ceiling.

"Giant pandas!" Miss Cactus snapped. "Giant pandas eat bamboo shoots, not elephants!" The inspector turned to Mrs Norton.

"Every lesson must have a purpose," she said. "It must be written down. We need to know what the aims of this task are. Well?" Miss Cactus eyeballed Mrs Norton.

"I thought the children might enjoy it," Mrs Norton said in a small voice.

"Enjoy?" Miss Cactus squeaked. She looked at the other inspectors with horror. "ENJOY? This is a SCHOOL! You're not supposed to enjoy it! It's not a, a, a chocolate biscuit! It's a school!"

Ross had begun to feel a bit sorry for Mrs Norton. He looked across at Katie and Charlie and pulled a face. If this was what things were going to be like with the inspectors, then he didn't think Mad Iris was going to go down very well at all.

Chapter 5

Where Do You Hide an Ostrich?

At last the inspectors left and went to visit another class in the school. Soon after that a message arrived from Mr Grimble. The message was marked "Top Secret" in big red letters. Mrs Norton read it and looked worried.

"I have a secret message from our head teacher," she told the class in a whisper. "It says, 'Don't let the inspectors see Mad Iris! They will go bananas – especially Miss

Cactus, who is allergic to animals of all kinds!'
Including humans," Mrs Norton added, and then
she blushed. "You didn't hear me say that," she
told the class.

"Yes we did," they answered.

"Oh dear," Mrs Norton said. "Then let's
make it a secret between us."

"We like secrets," Katie said, and the
class agreed. It was a secret. In fact, it was
becoming a very secretive kind of day.

"Yes, but the message has to stay secret
too," Ross said. He looked at Mrs Norton. "I
think you have to eat it to make sure it stays
secret," he told her.

"Really?" Mrs Norton looked at the
message. It didn't look in the least bit tasty.

"It's a secret," the class chanted. "You always have to eat secret messages after you've read them."

"Really?" Mrs Norton said again. "Oh dear."

She ate the message. The class watched her with wide eyes.

"She did it!" Ian Tufnell cried. "She ate the message! Wow!"

Everyone was very impressed. Mrs Norton looked a lot more cheerful as she swallowed the final bit of the message.

"There! It's all gone," she said.

"Mrs Norton's brilliant!" Kelly murmured. Everyone agreed, including Mrs Norton.

But just then another problem arrived. It was a very big, ostrich-sized problem. In fact, the problem *was* an ostrich. Mad Iris had escaped from her shed and was on the loose. The whole class saw her dash across the playground.

"We've got to catch her before the inspectors see her!" Ross cried. "Come on!"

And in the wink of an eye the whole class had rushed out to the playground and were chasing after Mad Iris.

Of course, Mad Iris thought it was a game and she liked games very much. She raced around pecking at the children and Mrs Norton too. She pecked at their shoe laces. She pecked at their hair. She pecked at Mrs Norton's bottom.

"Ooh!" Mrs Norton squeaked, and she jumped in the air. "Oh!" she squeaked as Mad Iris did it again. Mad Iris liked to make Mrs Norton squeak.

At last Katie and Charlie managed to get hold of the ostrich. They led her over to the classroom and they all went in.

Mad Iris liked the classroom a lot. It was full of lovely, chewy things.

"That's my pencil!" Gloria cried as the pencil disappeared into Mad Iris's beak.

"That's my workbook!" Kelly cried as the workbook went the same way.

"Here! She can eat my workbook too," Ian Tufnell said.

Then Iris saw the cardboard elephant. She lifted her head and eyeballed it.

"I think she wants to eat it," Katie murmured.

Mrs Norton was horrified. She almost threw herself in front of the elephant.

"No!" she shouted. She wagged a stern finger at Mad Iris. The ostrich took no notice. She just took a step towards Mrs Norton.

Just then Charlie shouted, "The inspectors are crossing the playground. They're heading straight for our classroom!"

Even Mad Iris turned and stared out of the window. For a moment everyone in the class froze. But not Mad Iris. She took the opportunity to have another quick peck at Mrs Norton's bottom.

"Ooh!" went Mrs Norton. "Ooh!"

And if ostriches can smile then that is what Mad Iris did. In fact, she grinned.

"What are we going to do?" Ross shouted.

Charlie's eyes sparkled. "Hide Iris in the elephant!" he said. "Come on, it's big enough. We can push her inside."

"But the inspectors will see her legs," Kelly Jessup pointed out.

"Everybody stand in front of the elephant," Mrs Norton ordered. "Come on, hurry! That will hide Mad Iris's legs from view."

It was a bit of a struggle to get Mad Iris inside the elephant, but they managed it. Just as the inspectors walked in, the whole class moved to stand in front of it.

Miss Cactus eyed them, one by one. She seemed to suspect something was up. Her eyes narrowed to slits.

"What ARE you doing?" she demanded.

"I am posing the children for a class photo in front of the cardboard elephant we have made," said Mrs Norton.

"Ah," muttered Mr Twine.

"I've got a photo of my children," said Mr Singh, and he reached for his family snap.

"But you don't have a camera, Mrs Norton," Miss Cactus pointed out.

"I haven't finished posing the children yet," Mrs Norton said.

"Hmmmm," Mr Twine murmured, and he looked up at the ceiling.

Miss Cactus sniffed. "Have you got the aims of this work written down yet?" she said.

"We are all working on that," Mrs Norton lied.

"Good. I want to see them by the end of the day," Miss Cactus said. She turned on her heel and all three inspectors headed for the door.

The class heaved a sigh of relief. Mrs Norton heaved a sigh of relief. Everything was going to be fine.

As Miss Cactus reached the door she turned back to the class. And that was when the big cardboard elephant began heading for the door too.

Chapter 6
Mad Iris Takes Charge!

Miss Cactus boggled. She wobbled and goggled, and still the elephant slid towards her. At last her nerve broke. She turned tail and fled.

"There's a cardboard elephant chasing me!" she yelled at Mr Twine and Mr Singh.

"Oh," said Mr Twine.

Mr Singh patted his pocket to make sure his children were safe.

Miss Cactus hurtled past them, still shouting. She headed straight for Mr Grimble's office and burst in past the door like a hand grenade. Mr Grimble almost fell off his chair.

"This school," Miss Cactus panted. "This school – *pant pant* – is a disaster area! *Pant pant*."

Mr Grimble sighed. "Oh dear," he said.

"Yes," Miss Cactus snapped. She had got her breath back now. "I have never seen such madness. I have just been chased across the playground by an elephant."

"What? I didn't think Captain Kapow was coming until tomorrow," Mr Grimble said.

"It was a cardboard elephant," Miss Cactus insisted.

Mr Grimble was beginning to think that maybe the "madness" was in Miss Cactus's head. A cardboard elephant that chased school inspectors?

"Surely cardboard elephants can't move?" he asked.

"Go and see for yourself!" Miss Cactus ordered.

So Mr Grimble went out to the playground and Miss Cactus followed. There was the elephant. Mr Grimble walked up to it with care. He thought it might try and charge him. But no, the elephant didn't budge.

And so Mr Grimble went right up to it and patted its side. He turned to Miss Cactus and raised his hands.

"It's cardboard," he said. "It's made from boxes. It can't move."

"I'm telling you it chased me," Miss Cactus repeated. "I want you to have it removed from this school at once."

Mr Grimble had just caught sight of something moving behind Miss Cactus. The head of an ostrich poked out from the corner of a classroom. A child's hand reached out and pulled it back, but then the head popped out again, followed by the body and the legs. Mad Iris was behind Miss Cactus and was running straight at her.

"I think you'd better move," Mr Grimble said.

"I am not moving until you sort out this elephant," Miss Cactus shouted. "I am not moving until –"

At that moment Mad Iris screeched to a halt right behind Miss Cactus. Her eyes glinted with delight and with one single peck the ostrich sent Miss Cactus jumping higher than if she'd been on a trampoline.

"Ow!" Miss Cactus yelled. "That was my *bottom*!" As she landed back on her feet she saw Mad Iris.

"An ostrich *and* an elephant! What kind of school is this? I'll see that you get closed down! And then I will report you to the police! Your school is a disgrace. It's a danger to the public!"

Miss Cactus hadn't even finished shouting at Mr Grimble when Mad Iris got fed up with the sound of the inspector's voice. The ostrich started pecking at Miss Cactus's ankles, and then her jacket and her hair. Last of all she grabbed hold of Miss Cactus's nose.

"Let go!" Miss Cactus ordered. So Mad Iris let go and grabbed her left knee instead.

Mr Twine and Mr Singh stood not far away and watched.

"Ah," Mr Twine muttered. He shook his head.

"Goodness me," Mr Singh said. He got out his photo of his children and looked at that. It seemed that their smiling faces helped to calm him down.

"Ow! Ow!" Miss Cactus yelled. "You'll pay for this!" she shouted at Mr Grimble. "The whole school will pay for this. You are in such trouble. I will be writing you the worst school report ever. Get this ostrich off me!"

But Mad Iris wouldn't stop. At last Miss Cactus made a run for it, over to the school gate. She reached the gate just as Mrs Fretting walked in.

"An ostrich!" Mrs Fretting cried. "My poor Charlie's allergic to ostriches! What's going on? Somebody save my Charlie!"

"Somebody save *me!*" Miss Cactus howled.

Mr Grimble watched them all in despair. He put his hands to his head. How many problems could he deal with? What should he do?

Save Charlie?

Save Miss Cactus?

Save the school?

Save himself?

It was all too, *too* much.

Poor Mr Grimble looked up the sky, squeezed his eyes tight shut and yelled.

"AAAAAAAARRRRRGGGGGGHHHHHHHHH!!!!"

Chapter 7
Problems in the Playground

The next day arrived. It brought thunder, lightning and heavy, *heavy* rain. It also brought the three inspectors *and* Mrs Fretting.

Mr Grimble saw them coming and tried to hide in his office, but Miss Cactus and Mrs Fretting almost broke the door down.

"We almost died yesterday!" Miss Cactus declared.

"Mad Iris is only an ostrich, she's not a hand grenade or a nuclear bomb," Mr Grimble pointed out. "And she only chased you, Miss Cactus. She didn't chase Mrs Fretting."

"Hmmm," Mr Twine said with a nod.

Mrs Fretting turned purple with anger. "I almost died *too*. I'm allergic to ostriches!"

"I thought it was Charlie who was allergic to ostriches," said Mr Grimble.

"He is, and I caught it off him."

"I don't think you can catch allergies, Mrs Fretting," Mr Grimble said. He felt very tired.

"Ah," Mr Twine said with a nod.

"My five children have no allergies, no allergies at all," Mr Singh said with a smile. "The secret is –"

But nobody heard what Mr Singh's secret was because Mrs Fretting was about to burst with rage. She turned to Miss Cactus.

"Listen to him!" she shouted. "That man thinks I'm *lying*! Me! He should be sacked from his job!"

"I agree," Miss Cactus sniped. "And I'm the one who is going to sack him."

But before Miss Cactus could sack Mr Grimble, she was interrupted by the arrival of Captain Kapow.

Or rather, CAPTAIN KAPOW!!

Captain Kapow was tall, dark and handsome. He had a dashing smile full of bright white teeth. He had a proper suntan that he'd picked up in Africa on safari. He had hair so dark it had to have come out of a bottle.

"Hello, ladies. Hello, head teacher," Captain Kapow said. His voice was like honey with a hint of chilli pepper. He had a twirly moustache and a battered safari hat.

Miss Cactus stared at Captain Kapow and gulped. "Oh!" she gasped. She sounded a bit like Mr Twine, only far less bored.

"Ooh!" Mrs Fretting murmured. She sounded like herself, only in a good mood. "I think I might faint into his arms. I'm allergic to tall, dark, handsome men. They make me swoon."

Captain Kapow smiled at everyone again. "I've brought the animals," he said. "Should I get them ready?"

"By all means," Mr Grimble said. "I shall go round the classes and gather the children."

Mr Grimble was very happy. Now he had a good excuse to escape from the clutches of Miss

Cactus and Mrs Fretting. They were far too busy admiring Captain Kapow.

Then Mrs Fretting and the inspectors all went and stood under the school porch to watch Captain Kapow unload his animals. It was pouring with rain and the animals didn't like it much.

Two monkeys chattered at each other and covered their heads with their small hairy hands. An eagle owl blinked a lot and went "whoo-hoo" in protest. A little crocodile didn't care about the rain at all. A box full of meerkats all stood on their back legs as if they hoped someone would pass round some umbrellas.

At last Captain Kapow lifted out a snake. It was a python, a great big python. Captain Kapow let the snake coil around him.

Miss Cactus gasped. "He's the bravest man I've ever seen!" she whispered to Mrs Fretting.

It was at that point that there was a gigantic flash of lightning followed by a ginormous explosion of thunder and the rain turned into the Niagara Falls.

The animals hooted and barked and squawked in fear. The monkeys banged against their little cage and all of a sudden the door sprang open and they were out. They ran straight into the meerkats' box and overturned it. The meerkats shot out and scattered in all directions. Then the monkeys managed to set free the little crocodile.

Captain Kapow charged round trying to catch all the animals. This upset the python and it slid off the Captain and made straight for Miss Cactus.

"Save me, Captain Kapow!!" Miss Cactus cried.

"I'm rather busy wrestling a crocodile!" Captain Kapow shouted back.

"Oh!" said Mr Twine.

"Whoo-hoo," said the eagle owl.

"At least my children are safe," said Mr Singh, and he patted his pocket.

The monkeys were now trying to climb up Mrs Fretting.

"I'm being eaten by monkeys," she screamed. "Someone save me. I'm allergic to being eaten by monkeys!"

So there it was.

Miss Cactus was about to be squeezed to death by the python. Mrs Fretting was about to be dinner for the monkeys. And all the while, the storm raged on. Lightning flashed in all directions. A new thunder roll started even before the last thunder roll had finished. The playground was covered in animals and children and everyone was racing around so much it was impossible to know who was chasing what or what was chasing who.

"Call the Fire Brigade!" Miss Cactus yelled, as the python slithered over her feet and curled around her legs. "Call the police! Call the ambulance! Call the lifeboats!"

And then, at last, the Rescue Service arrived. What was the Rescue Service? Well, in fact it was Mad Iris, and riding on Mad Iris's back were Charlie and Ross and Katie. Behind them came the whole of Mrs Norton's class, including Mrs Norton and Mr Grimble too.

Mad Iris kicked at the crocodile until it just gave up and lay down. Then Mad Iris rocketed off towards Miss Cactus.

"No! No!" Miss Cactus screamed when she saw Mad Iris *and* the python making for her.

Peck! Peck! Peck! went Mad Iris at the python's head. The snake gave a loud hiss and

slithered back to Captain Kapow, who was now sitting in a big puddle and crying. His twirly moustache had gone very droopy indeed and rainwater was trickling off both ends of it. (Mad Iris had already eaten his safari hat.)

Next, Mad Iris had a go at the two monkeys and chased them back into their cage. Ross shut the door on them. Then Mad Iris picked up the meerkats one by one in her beak and popped them back in their box. Katie put the lid on top.

Charlie picked up the rather small and gloomy crocodile and slipped that back in its cage too.

And that was that. Job done.

Chapter 8

The End – and Mrs Norton Does Some Colouring

Miss Cactus was in tears.

"I am *so* grateful!" she told Mr Grimble. "That ostrich of yours saved our lives."

"Yes, she did," said Mr Grimble, who was very proud.

Mrs Fretting was staring at Charlie. "You rode an ostrich, Charlie!" she said. "But, but, but – you're allergic to ostriches!"

Charlie looked at his mother. "Mum," he began. "I'm not allergic to anything. You just think I am."

"Oh!" said Mrs Fretting.

"Oh," murmured Mr Twine.

"Well, there's a turn up for the book," said Mrs Fretting. "No allergies at all. I'm very pleased to hear it. So I don't have to hide you under my coat when we see a door?"

"No, Mum," Charlie said with a grin.

"And you're not allergic to reading?"

"I love reading," Charlie declared. "Reading is what I like best."

"Ah," said Mr Twine. "That's nice."

Miss Cactus stared at Mr Twine. "You spoke!" she said. "Two words!"

Mr Twine frowned. "Hmmm," he hmmmed.

Then all the grown-ups went off for a cup of tea and a slice of cake in the staffroom. And the children had to sit in their classrooms and get ever so bored because it was wet play.

At least they weren't bored for long, thanks to Mad Iris. She decided to go round all the classrooms eating their pencils and trying to tug Ian Tufnell's hair off his head.

At the end of the day the children showed the school inspectors their work. They had written stories about Mad Iris and about Captain Kapow's visit. They had painted pictures and written poems and made little books to show their work.

The inspectors were very impressed and they said that Pudding Lane was one of the best schools they had ever been to. Then they went home to write up a very good report, and Mr Grimble breathed a sigh of relief.

And that's the end, almost. But you see, when the children wrote their stories about the storm and the animals escaping not one of them said anything about how horrible Miss Cactus had been. They were very polite children, after all.

It was Mrs Norton who wrote the true story of the inspectors' visit. You see, Mrs Norton kept a secret diary and every day she wrote things in it. On this particular day she wrote exactly what she thought of Miss Cactus and how nasty and prickly the inspector had been. Mrs Norton drew pictures too, and her favourite picture showed the python squeezing Miss Cactus and Mad Iris pulling her nose at the same time. Mrs Norton even coloured it in.

Our books are tested
for children and young people by
children and young people.

Thanks to everyone who consulted on
a manuscript for their time and effort in
helping us to make our books better
for our readers.